Hopes and dreams for:

_____

_____

For Dougie and Billy
~ H.E.

For Florence and Henry x
~ H.G.

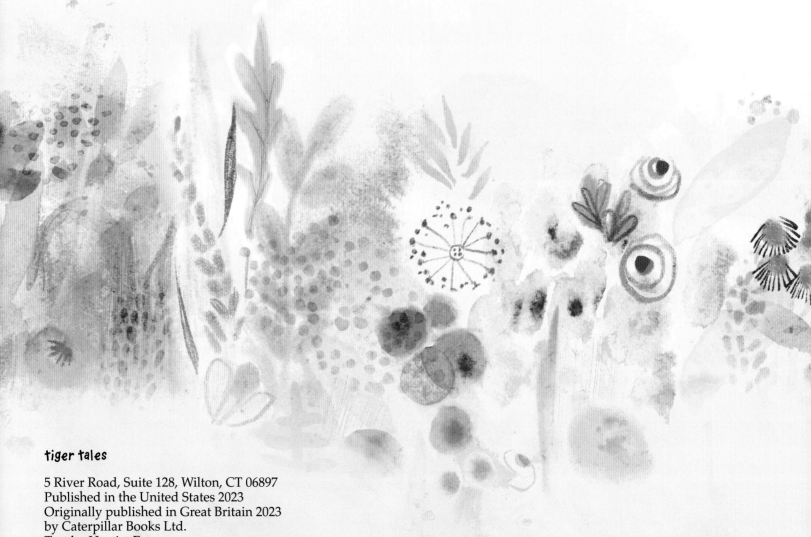

tiger tales

5 River Road, Suite 128, Wilton, CT 06897
Published in the United States 2023
Originally published in Great Britain 2023
by Caterpillar Books Ltd.
Text by Harriet Evans
Text copyright © 2023 Caterpillar Books Ltd.
Illustrations copyright © 2023 Heidi Griffiths
ISBN-13: 978-1-6643-0013-2
ISBN-10: 1-6643-0013-9
Printed in China
CPB/2800/2231/0722
10 9 8 7 6 5 4 3 2 1

www.tigertalesbooks.com

All Your Tomorrows

by
HARRIET EVANS

tiger tales

Illustrated by
HEIDI GRIFFITHS

I cradle **you**,
small slip of a creature.
Barely the length of my
forearm. In this body,
so **warm** and **new**,
you hold a history
yet to happen.

Your fingers fold around a future that I can only dream of.

How can something so small carry something so big?

These legs
will scramble over
mountains,

wade through
waters and wander
the world.

Run,

leap,

and **bound**
until your
muscles
burn.

You are a **wild** thing.
Let no one tame
your stride.

These knees, now soft and creased like rumpled linen, will become a patchwork of memories.

Each scrape and bruise a **testament** to trees climbed and **adventures** had.

Battle scars that promise, though you may fall, you will **still** get back up.

These feet will **root** you to the places you'll call **home.**

I hope you'll **sink** your toes into sand, leaving footprints in those beads of sunshine.

I hope you'll feel the
squish of mud,
prehistoric
oozing,

and the **crisp**
crackle of amber
leaves under
your steps.

These arms will lift, carry, and push.

I want you to know your power.
The world might weigh you down, but it will never crush you.

This hair — a song from generations past — now writes itself on your skin.

Tousled lion mane
that roars your wildness...

...or tamed to
proclaim the early
morning love of tired
fingers fumbling
through braids.

These eyes,
so wide and bright.
What will they see?

Keep your
curiosity close
to you—steel on
which to sharpen
your own **point
of view.**

The sparks will
light up the darkest
of nights.

These ears
that will catch the
melodies of others.

Let their music pour into
you until your **heart**
is an **orchestra**.

This mouth
with its smiles on which
already I hang my heart
like a familiar coat rack.

Laugh with life, but
don't be afraid to shout.

You have the right
to be heard.

These hands

that will sometimes speak
louder than words ever could.

I'll teach them different languages:

touch, creation,
kindness.

The world spins on its axis
like clay on a potter's wheel,

ready for you to
shape and mold.

This **nose** that
will breathe in **life**
by the lungful.

Inhale the sea's coarse tang, the sharp scent of pines...

...and the heady welcome of flowers.

This **heart** that will buoy
you up, that will sometimes feel,
even in a body as powerful as
yours, too **large** to contain.

How can something
so small carry
something
so big?